D0682323

This Book Belongs To:

This is a Parragon Book
This edition published in 2007

Parragon
Queen Street House,
4 Queen Street, BATH BA1 1HE, UK

This book was created by small world creations ltd

Printed in China

ISBN 978-1-4054-1596-5

Polly the Potty Postlady

p

Polly Postlady worked hard delivering letters, and she was always in a hurry. She hated to keep the people on her round waiting - and Mr Price the Postmaster always expected her back at the post office by 12 o'clock.

One morning Polly was in a bigger hurry than ever.
She had overslept and was late for work!

"Hurry, hurry, rush and hurry!" Polly muttered to herself as she rushed out the door.

"People are waiting for their letters!" Polly Postlady said to herself, as she sped to the post office on her bike.

"And Mr Price will be waiting for me!"

She zoomed down the street
as fast as she could go.

"Sorry I'm late, Mr Price," Polly puffed
as she flew through the post office door.
"Good morning,
Polly!" said Mr Price.
"Your postbag is
all ready
- and it looks
very full today!"

"Thanks, Mr Price," said Polly.
"I'll really have to hurry, with all those letters and parcels!"

Polly sped down Main Street and tore around the corner of Jackson Road.

She was going so fast that she didn't see the removal van in front of her until it was too late!

"LOOK OUT!"
shouted the removal men.

'Oh deeeeeeaaaaar!"
shouted Polly, as she went flying off her bike.

Everything in Polly's postbag went flying, too!

"Oh no! It will take ages to collect all these!" cried Polly, when she had stood up and dusted herself off. "And I'm in such a hurry today!"

The removal men helped Polly collect all the letters, postcards, and parcels and put them back in her bag. It wasn't too long before she was ready to go.

But when Polly picked up her bike, she saw that the tyre was flat! "I've got a puncture!" she cried. "I can't ride this now. What will I do?"

"You'll have to walk your round today, Polly," said one of the removal men. "Oh no!" said Polly. "I'm late enough as it is! I'd better get going!"

And she ran off down the road.

Polly ran off to
deliver the post
as quickly
as she could.

But she was in such a
hurry that she got
all the names
and addresses
mixed up!

Mr Green, on Jackson Road,
was expecting a
parcel of books.

Instead, he got two letters
and a gas bill addressed
Mrs Jackson!

Mrs Jackson, who lived on Holly Drive, got a magazine that was supposed to go to Holly Walker!

And Holly Walker, who lived on Green Street, got the parcel of books meant for Mr Green!

Everybody was terribly confused, especially Polly Postlady!

"I must be going **potty**!" she exclaimed.

Polly rushed and hurried as quickly
as she could to try and sort everything out...

... but by eleven o'clock her postbag was still half full.

She was beginning to feel hopeless, when suddenly she saw something that gave her a brilliant idea.

"Jack, may I borrow your skateboard, please?"
Polly asked one of the children.

"I promise to return it as soon as I've delivered all my letters."
"Sure, Polly," said Jack.

Polly had never been
on a skateboard
before, but she
bravely stepped on.

Polly wibbled

and wobbled ...

... and teetered and tottered ...

... then she skidded and swayed ...

... and WHOOOOOSHED

and WHIZZZZZZED

down the street

"Wheeeeeeeee!" cried Polly with glee. "This is just what I need!"

"I'm back, Mr Price!" she gasped, tripping over her bike as she staggered through the door. "Right on time!"

"I'm glad, Polly," said Mr Price. "And I'm glad you're all right. The removal men brought back your bike and told me about your accident this morning. I guess we'll have to mend that puncture right away."

"Oh there's no hurry, Mr Price," said Polly.

"I think I've found a much better form of transport for a potty postlady like me!